GREEDY ZEBRA

Books written by Mwenye Hadithi and illustrated by Adrienne Kennaway

Greedy Zebra
Hot Hippo
Crafty Chameleon (winner of the Kate Greenaway Medal 1987)
Tricky Tortoise

British Library Cataloguing in Publication Data

Hadithi, Mwenye
    Greedy zebra.
    I. Title   II. Kennaway, Adrienne
    823'.914(J)   PZ7
    ISBN 0-340-32892-4

First published 1984
Sixth impression 1989

Published by Hodder and Stoughton Children's Books,
a division of Hodder and Stoughton Ltd,
Mill Road, Dunton Green, Sevenoaks, Kent TN13 2YA

Printed in Belgium by Proost International Book Production

GREEDY ZEBRA

by **Mwenye Hadithi**

Illustrated by **Adrienne Kennaway**

HODDER AND STOUGHTON
LONDON SYDNEY AUCKLAND TORONTO

Long, long ago, all the animals in the world
were a dull, depressing colour; no coats, no horns,
no spots and no stripes. Just dull and dusty. Until . . .

One stormy day in the heart of the leafy forests of Africa
there was a great rumbling in the earth, and all
of a sudden a huge cave appeared in the ground.
A few of the animals crept cautiously up
to this new and wonderful sight, and when
the bravest of them peered into the
darkness he saw something glittering
                    amongst the rocks.

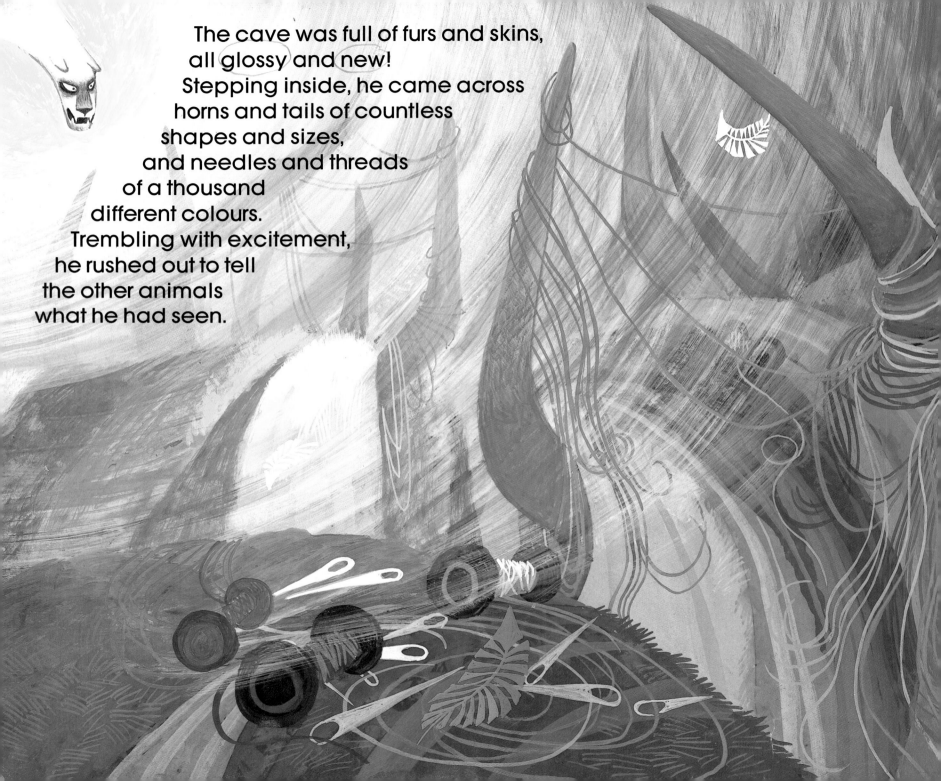

The cave was full of furs and skins,
all glossy and new!
Stepping inside, he came across
horns and tails of countless
shapes and sizes,
and needles and threads
of a thousand
different colours.
Trembling with excitement,
he rushed out to tell
the other animals
what he had seen.

The news spread far and wide, and soon all the animals
were on their way to see the cave, running and jumping
and sliding and swinging,
and slithering through the trees.

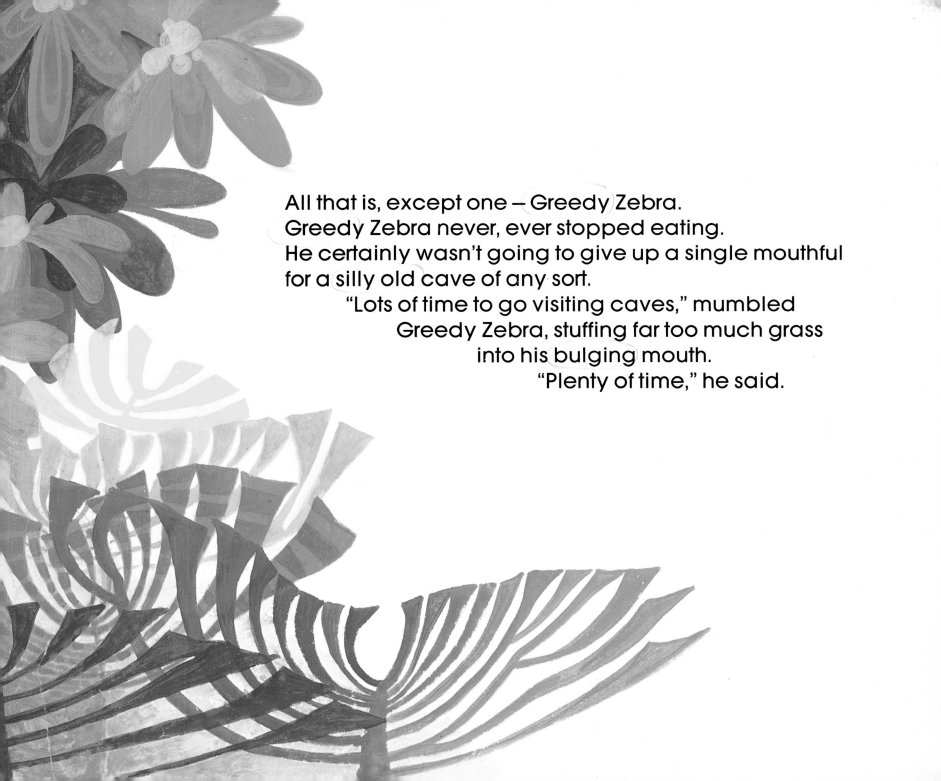

All that is, except one – Greedy Zebra.
Greedy Zebra never, ever stopped eating.
He certainly wasn't going to give up a single mouthful
for a silly old cave of any sort.
"Lots of time to go visiting caves," mumbled
Greedy Zebra, stuffing far too much grass
into his bulging mouth.
"Plenty of time," he said.

Soon all the animals in the jungle were gathered at the mouth of the cave, waiting for Elephant to speak. Elephant was the one who knew everything because Eagle told him all the secrets of the Spirit of the Mists. He coughed pompously, and addressed the gathering. "It is time for you all to have coats," he said. "There are all kinds of materials here from which you may choose. You will be issued with needles by Rabbit, but there is only one needle each, so take good care of it. Now you may go in — but no shoving and pushing, and keep in an orderly line!"

Meanwhile, Greedy Zebra was still eating. "Munch, munch," he went.
"This particular grass is so delicious…" He stopped to gape
at the beautiful thing in front of him. It couldn't
be! But it was
Sable the antelope,
and she was
wearing the most
glorious new coat.
And horns!
She was
wearing
horns!

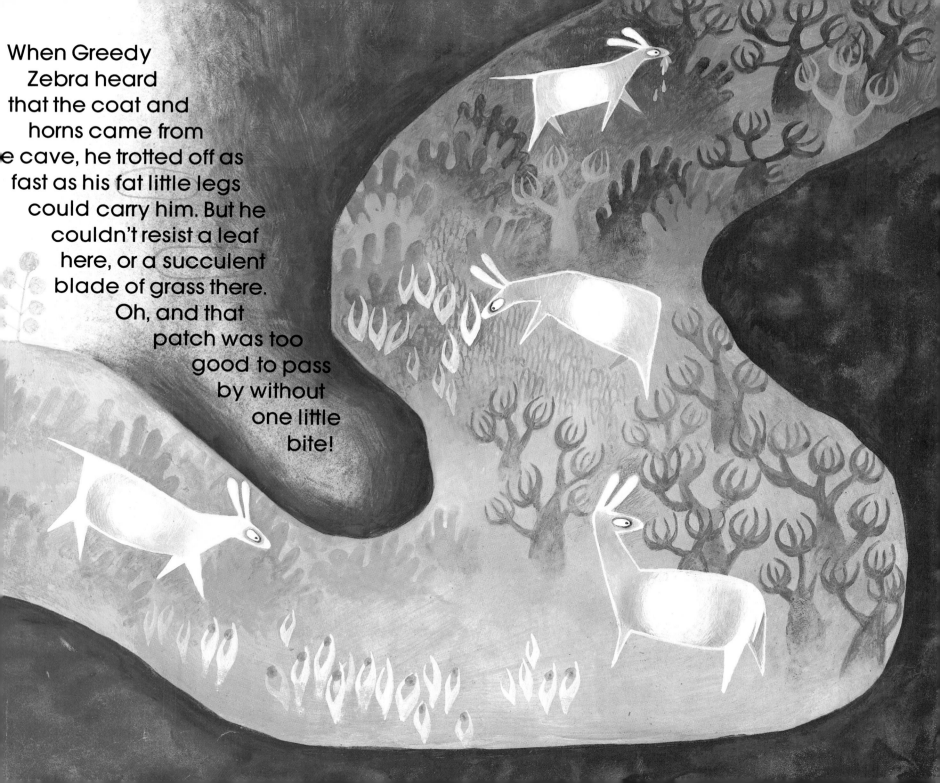

When Greedy
Zebra heard
that the coat and
horns came from
the cave, he trotted off as
fast as his fat little legs
could carry him. But he
couldn't resist a leaf
here, or a succulent
blade of grass there.
Oh, and that
patch was too
good to pass
by without
one little
bite!

From time to time he met another, and another,

and yet another,

of the wonderfully clothed animals. Stopping for a last bite not far from the cave, he watched Leopard finish her sewing. Leopard, as careful as usual, had sewn the most splendid fur coat with spots all over it. Greedy Zebra could hardly believe his eyes as he watched Leopard wriggle into the perfectly fitting fur.

"I shall have spots like that," he said to himself, and he hurried off, eager to reach the cave.

But it was
a hot day, so
he stopped for a
cool drink
at a stream
and there he came
across a patch
of the greenest grass
he had ever seen.
"Delicious," he munched,
smacking his chubby lips.

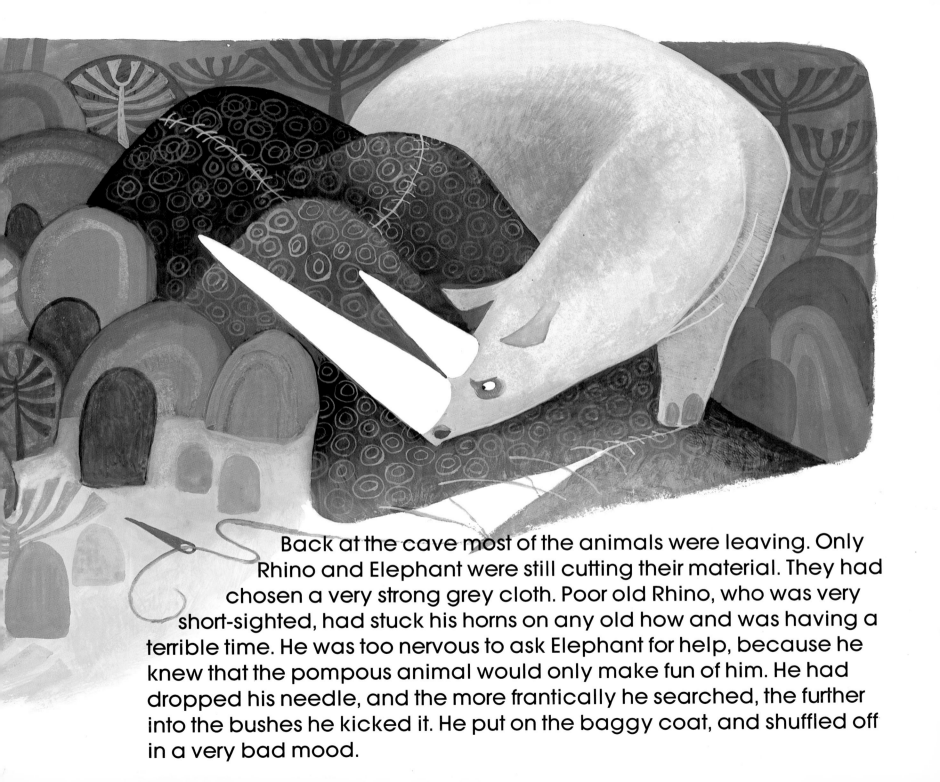

Back at the cave most of the animals were leaving. Only
Rhino and Elephant were still cutting their material. They had
chosen a very strong grey cloth. Poor old Rhino, who was very
short-sighted, had stuck his horns on any old how and was having a
terrible time. He was too nervous to ask Elephant for help, because he
knew that the pompous animal would only make fun of him. He had
dropped his needle, and the more frantically he searched, the further
into the bushes he kicked it. He put on the baggy coat, and shuffled off
in a very bad mood.

Just then Greedy Zebra trotted by,
with blades of grass bulging from his mouth.
"I'll have spots like Leopard," he was saying.
"and horns like Kudu, a mane like Lion and
a tail like Cheetah. I shall be the
finest looking animal in the
forest!"

And at the risk of indigestion he gave a short gallop into the cave. Then he stopped, aghast.

There was nothing left! No horns, no fine cloth — nothing.
Frantically he searched through the cave, but all he
could find were a few strips of black material.
Forlornly he cut them all to the same size and stitched
them together.

"It looks very tight," he thought nervously to himself. Being such a very fat zebra, he had a terrible time squeezing into his coat. He pushed and grunted and oohed and aahed and – pop, he was inside it. But what a tight fit! It was nearly bursting at the seams around his fat tummy. He trotted down to the stream to take a quick bite of a leafy bush – and POP, his coat burst open.

POP!

POP!
POP!

His tubby tummy
squeezed through
the seams.
How the monkeys
roared with
laughter!

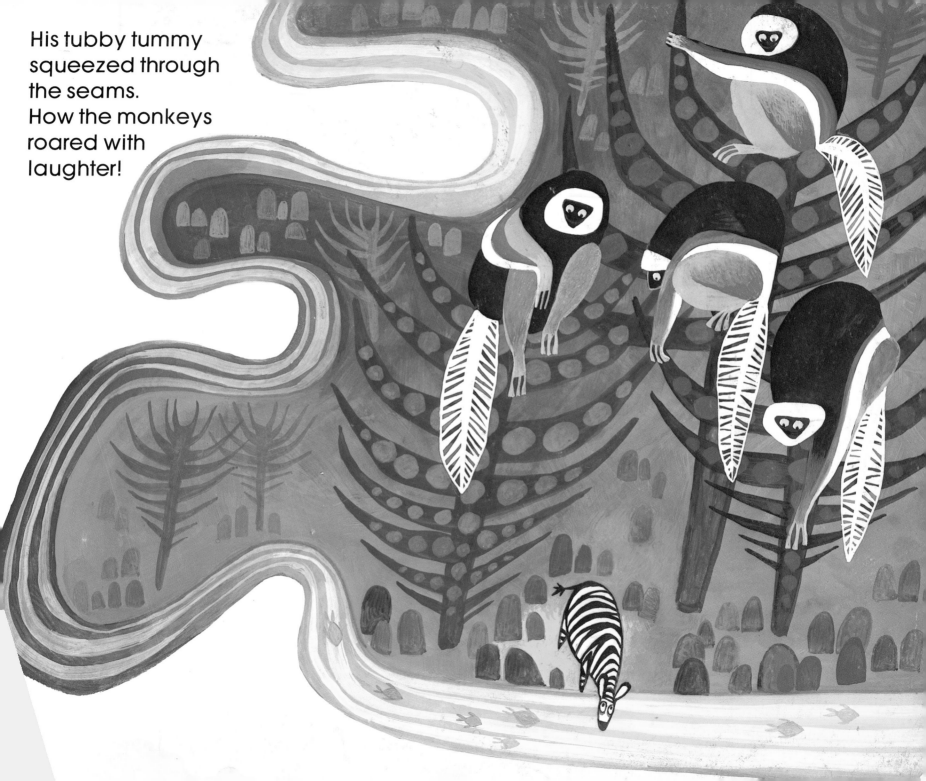

To this day his chubby
stomach shines through
his coat because
he is so greedy.

PRINTED IN BELGIUM BY
proost
INTERNATIONAL BOOK PRODUCTION